Silas Weir Mitchell

**The Mother**

And other Poems

Silas Weir Mitchell

**The Mother**
*And other Poems*

ISBN/EAN: 9783744770286

Printed in Europe, USA, Canada, Australia, Japan

Cover: Foto ©Andreas Hilbeck / pixelio.de

More available books at **www.hansebooks.com**

# THE MOTHER
# AND OTHER POEMS

BY

## S. WEIR MITCHELL, M. D., LL. D. HARV.

AUTHOR OF "A PSALM OF DEATHS AND OTHER POEMS," ETC.

BOSTON AND NEW YORK
HOUGHTON, MIFFLIN AND COMPANY
The Riverside Press, Cambridge
1893

*The Riverside Press, Cambridge, Mass., U. S. A.*
Electrotyped and Printed by H. O. Houghton & Co.

# CONTENTS.

|  | Page |
|---|---|
| The Mother | 1 |
| Responsibility | 12 |
| The Roman Campagna | 20 |
| The Protestant Cemetery at Rome | 23 |
| Roma | 26 |
| My Lady of the Roses | 29 |
| The Quaker Lady | 34 |
| The Wreck of the Emmeline | 38 |
| Venice | 45 |
| Venice to Italy | 46 |
| The Decay of Venice | 47 |
| Pisa : The Duomo | 48 |
| The Vestal's Dream | 49 |
| Lincoln | 50 |
| The Lost Philopena | 51 |
| St. Christopher | 52 |
| Dreamland | 55 |
| Evening by the Sea | 58 |
| Idleness | 59 |
| A Graveyard | 60 |
| Loss | 61 |

iv CONTENTS

COME IN . . . . .

GOOD-NIGHT . . . . .

THE RISING TIDE . . .

VERSES . . . . . .

*" I will incline mine ear to the parable, and show my dark
speech upon the harp."*

CHRISTMAS! Christmas! merry Christmas!
    rang the bells. O God of grace!
In the stillness of the death-room motionless I
    kept my place,
While beneath my eyes a wanness came upon
    the little face,
And an empty smile that stung me, as the pallor
    grew apace.
Then, as if from some far distance, spake a
    voice: " The child is dead."
" Dead?" I cried. " Is God not good? What
    thing accursed is that you said?"
Swift I searched their eyes of pity, swaying,
    bowed, and all my soul,
Shrunken as a hand had crushed it, crumpled
    like a useless scroll
Read and done with, passed from sorrows: only
    with me lingered yet

Some dim sense of easeful comfort in the glad
  leave to forget.
But again life's scattered fragments, memories
  of joy and woe,
Tremulously came to oneness, as a storm-torn
  lake may grow
Quiet, winning back its pictures, when the wild
  winds cease to blow.
As if called for God's great audit came a vision
  of my years,
Broken gleams of youth and girlhood, all the
  woman's love and tears.
Marveling, myself I saw as one another sees,
  and smiled,
Crooning o'er my baby dolls, — part a mother,
  part a child;
Then, half sorry, ceased to wonder why I left
  my silent brood,
Till the lessoning years went by me, and the in-
  stinct, love-renewed,
Stirred again life's stronger fibre, and were
  mine these living things;
Bone of my bone! flesh of my flesh! Who on
  earth a title brings
Flawless as this mother-title, free from aught of
  mortal stain,

Innocent and pure possession, double-born of
    joy and pain?

Oh, what wonder these could help me, set me
    laughing, though I sobbed

As they drew my very heart out, and the laden
    breasts were robbed!

Tender buds of changeful pleasure came as come
    the buds of May,

Trivial, wondrous, unexpected, blossoming from
    day to day.

Ah! the clutch of tendril-fingers, that with
    nature's cunning knew

So to coil in sturdy grapple round the stem
    from which they grew.

Shall a man this joy discover? How the heart-
    wine to the brain

Rushed with shock of bliss when, startled, first
    I won this simple gain!

How I mocked those seeking fingers, eager for
    their earliest toy,

Telling none my new-found treasure! Miser of
    the mother's joy,

Quick I caught the first faint ripple, answering
    me with lip and eyes,

As I stooped with mirthful purpose, keen to
    capture fresh replies;

Oh, the pretty wonder of it, when was born the
    art to smile,
Or the new, gay trick of laughter filled my eyes
    with tears the while, —
Helpful tears, love's final language, when the
    lips no more can say,
Tears, like kindly prophets, warning of another,
    darker day.
Thus my vision lost its gladness, and I stood on
    life's dim strand,
Watching where a little love-bark drifted slowly
    from the land ;
For again the bells seemed ringing Christmas
    o'er the snow of dawn,
And my dreaming memory hurt me with a hot
    face, gray and drawn,
And with small hands locked in anguish.  Ah!
    those days of helpless pain !
Mine the mother's wrathful sorrow.  Ah! my
    child, hadst thou been Cain,
Father of the primal murder, black with every
    hideous thought,
Cruel were the retribution ; for, alas ! what
    good is wrought
When the very torture ruins all the fine machine
    of thought ?

So with reeling brain I questioned, while the
    fevered cheek grew white,
And at last I seemed to pass with him, released,
    to outer night.
Seraph voices whispered round me. " God," they
    said, " hath set our task, —
Thou to question, we to answer : fear not ; ask
    what thou wouldst ask."
Wildly beat my heart. Thought only, regnant,
    held its sober pace,
Whilst, a wingèd mind, I wandered in the bleak
    domain of space.
Then I sought and saw untroubled all the mys-
    tery of time,
Where beneath me rolled the earth-star in its
    first chaotic slime,
As bewildering ages passing with their cyclic
    changes came,
Heaving land and 'whelming waters, ice and
    fierce volcanic flame,
Sway and shock of tireless atoms, pulsing with
    the throb of force,
Whilst the planet, rent and shaken, fled upon
    its mighty course.
Last, with calm of wonder hushed, I saw amid
    the surging strife

Rise the first faint stir of being and the tardy
    morn of life, —

Life in countless generations.  Speechless, mer-
    cilessly dumb,

Swept by ravage of disaster, tribe on tribe in
    silence come,

Till the yearning sense found voices, and on
    hill, and shore, and plain,

Dreary from the battling myriads rose the birth-
    right wail of pain.

God of pity!  Son of sorrows!  Wherefore
    should a will unseen

Launch on years of needless anguish this great
    agonized machine?

Was Himself who willed this torment but a
    slave to law self-made?

Or had some mad angel-demon here, unchecked
    and undismayed,

Leave to make of earth a Job; until the cruel
    game was played

Free to whirl the spinning earth-toy where his
    despot forces wrought,

While he watched each sense grow keener as
    the lifted creature bought

With the love-gift added sorrow, and there came
    to man's estate

Will, the helpless, thought, the bootless, all the
    deathward war with fate ?
Had this lord of trampled millions joy or grief,
    when first the mind,
Awful prize of contests endless, rose its giant
    foes to bind ;
When his puppet tamed the forces that had
    helped its birth to breed,
And with growth of wisdom master, trained
    them to its growing need ;
Last, upon the monster turning, on the serpent
    form of Pain,
Cried, " Bring forth no more in anguish ; " with
    the arrows of the brain
Smote this brute thing that no use had save to
    teach him to refrain
When earth's baser instincts tempted, and the
    better thought was vain ?
Then my soul one harshly answered, " Thou
    hast seen the whole of earth,
All its boundless years of misery, yea, its glad-
    ness and its mirth,
Yet thou hast a life created !  Hadst thou not
    a choice ?  Why cast
Purity to life's mad chances, where defeat is sure
    at last ? "

Low I moaned, " My tortured baby," and a
　　　gentler voice replied,
" One alone thy soul can answer, — this, this
　　　only, is denied.
Yet take counsel of thy sadness.　Should God
　　　give thy will a star
Freighted with eternal pleasure, free from agony
　　　and war,
Wouldst thou wish it ?　Think !　Time is not
　　　for the souls who roam in space.
Speak !　Thy will shall have its way.　Be
　　　mother of one joyous race.
Choose !　Yon time-worn world beneath thee
　　　thou shalt people free from guilt.
There nor pain nor death shall ruin, never there
　　　shall blood be spilt."
Then I trembled, hesitating, for I saw its beauty
　　　born,
Saw a Christ-like world of beings where no
　　　beast by beast was torn,
Where the morrows bred no sorrows, and the
　　　gentle knew not scorn.
" Yet," I said, " if life have meaning, and man
　　　must be, what shall lift
These but born for joy's inaction, these who
　　　crave no added gift ?

Let the world you bid me people hurl forever
    through the gloom,
Tenantless, a blasted record of some huge fu-
    nereal doom,
Sad with unremembered slaughter, but a cold
    and lonely tomb."


Deep and deeper grew the stillness, and I knew
    how vain my quest.
Not by God's supremest angel is that awful se-
    cret guessed.
Yet with dull reiteration, like the pendulum's
    dead throb,
Beat my heart; a moaning infant, all my body
    seemed to sob,
And a voice like to my baby's called to me
    across the night
As the darkness fell asunder, and I saw a wall
    of light
Barred with crucificial shadows, whence a weary
    wind did blow
Shuddering. I felt it pass me heavy with its
    freight of woe.
Said a voice, " Behold God's dearest ; also these
    no answer know.

These be they who paid in sorrow for the right
    to bid thee hear.
Had their lives in ease been cradled, had they
    never known a tear,
Feebly had their psalms of warning fallen upon
    the listening ear.
God the sun is God the shadow; and where
    pain is, God is near.
Take again thy life and use it with a sweetened
    sense of fear;
God is Father! God is Mother! Regent of a
    growing soul,
Free art thou to grant mere pleasure, free to
    teach it uncontrol.
Time is childhood! larger manhood bides be-
    yond life's sunset hour,
Where far other foes are waiting; and with ever
    gladder power,
Still the lord of awful choice, O striving crea-
    ture of the sod,
Thou shalt learn that imperfection is the noblest
    gift of God!
For they mock his ample purpose who but
    dream, beyond the sky,

Of a heaven where will may slumber, and the
    trained decision die
In the competence of answer found in death's
    immense reply."


Then my vision passed, and weeping, lo! I woke,
    of death bereft;
At my breast the baby brother, yonder there
    the dead I left.
For my heart two worlds divided: his, my lost
    one's; his, who pressed
Closer, waking all the mother, as he drew the
    aching breast,
While twain spirits, joy and sorrow, hovered
    o'er my plundered nest.

NEWPORT, *October*, 1891.

# RESPONSIBILITY

Thus, lying among the roses in the garden of the Great Inn,
sang Attar El Din of things yet to be, when the Angels of
Affirmation and Denial should struggle for the soul of him
dead.

" I MOONKIR, the angel, am come
To count of his good deeds the sum,
For this mortal, death-stricken and dumb."

"I Nekkeer, the clerk of ill thought,
Am here to dispute what hath wrought
This maker of song, come to naught.

" Let us call from the valleys of gloom,
From the night graves of sleep and the tomb,
The wretched he lured to their doom."

Said Moonkir, the angel of light,
"Life is made of the day and the night;
Let us summon the souls he set right."

(12)

Then, parting the dark tents of sleep,
Or stirred from their earth-couches deep,
Came souls that were glad or did weep.

*Spake a Voice:*

" I sat beside the cistern on the sand,
When this man's song did take me in its hand,
And hurled me helpless, as a sling the stone
That knows not will or pity of its own.
Within my heart was seed of murder sown,
So once I struck, — yea, twice, when he did
    groan."

" Ay, that was the song," said a voice,
" Which I heard as I lay
'Gainst my camel's broad flanks,
Thinking how to repay
The death-debt, ere night fled away.
And I rose as he sang, to rejoice
With a blessing of thanks,
For the song took my slack will and me
As a strong man might lustily throw
The power of hand and of knee
To string up to purpose a bow.
Quick I stole through the dark, but was stayed,

Just to hear how, with every-day phrase,
Such as useth a child or a maid,
From praise of decision to praise
Of the quiet of evening, he fell,
As a brook groweth still on the plain
To picture how come through the grain
The women with jars to the well.
Near I drew o'er the sands cool and gray
With my knife in my teeth, swift to slay.
Hot and wet felt my hand as I crept;
Blank-eyed 'neath my eyes the man lay;
This other had struck where he slept."

Then Moonkir, who treasures good deeds,
To mark how the total exceeds,
Said, " He soweth of millet and weeds

" Who casts forth a song in the night,
As a pigeon is flung for its flight,
He knoweth not where 't will alight.

" Lo, Allah a wind doth command,
And the caravan dies in the sand,
And the good ship is sped to the land."

*Spake a Voice:*

" I lay among the idle on the grass,
And saw before me come and go, alas!
This evil rhymer.   And he sang how God
Is but the cruel user of the rod,
And how the wine cup better is than prayer ;
Whereon I cursed, and counseled with despair,
And drank with him, and left my field untilled:
So all my house with want and woe was filled."

*Spake a Voice:*

" And I, that took no heed of things divine,
And ever loved to loiter with the wine,
Was stirred to think, and straightway sobered
       went,
And in the folded stillness of my tent
Struggled with Allah, and at morning fair
Beheld this poet like the rest in prayer."

Cried he whose proportion of sin
These angels considered within,
Cried the soul of this **Attar El Din**,

" O weigher of goodness and light,
O stern clerk of evil and night,
Between the slow comings and flight

" Of the sun and the day-death there lies,
Ere sleep shall have cloaked a man's eyes,
Ere the red dawn shall bid him arise,

" An hour when the prayer seed is strown;
Man tilleth or letteth alone,
For the ground where it falls is his own.

" Behold at even-time within my tent
I wailed in song because a death-shaft, sent
From Azrael's bow, had laid again in dust
My eldest born; I sang because I must.
For hate, love, joy, or grief, like Allah's birds,
I have but song, and man's dull use of words
Fills not the thirsty cup of my desire
To hurt my brothers with the scorch of fire
That burns within.   Yea, they must share my
          fate,
Love with me, hate, with me be desolate;
And so I drew my bowstring to the eye,
And shot my shafts, I cared not where or why,
If but the men indifferent, who lay
Beneath the palm-trees at the fall of day,
I could make see with me the dead boy's look
That swayed me like the bent reeds of the brook.

" But one who heard, and through long stress
     of grief
Wrestled with agony of loss in vain,
Into the desert went, and made full brief
A clearance with the creditor called Pain,
And by a sword thrust gave his heart relief.

" One whose dry eyes were as the summer sand
Wept as I sang, and said, ' I understand.'

" And one who loved did also comprehend,
Because I sang how, to life's bitter end,
The death-fear sweetens love ; and went his way
With deepened love to where the dark-eyed
     lay."

*Spake a Voice :*
" My father's foe, a dying man,
Thirst-stricken by the brookside lay ;
Its prattle mocked him as it ran
So near, and yet so far away.
The cold, quick waters soothed my feet,
Hot from the long day's desert heat ;
I drank deep draughts, and deep delight
Of sated vengeance.  Life grew sweet

Because the great breast heaved and groaned,
The red eyes yearned, the black lips moaned,
Because my foe should die ere night.
Then, as a rich man scatters alms,
A careless singer 'neath the palms,
With lapse and laughter, and pauses long,
Merrily squandered the gold of song.
Just a babble of simple childish chants :
How they dig little wells with the small brown
      hand ;
How they watch the caravan march of the ants,
And build tall mosques with the shifting sand,
And are mighty sheiks of a corner of land.

" Ah ! the rush, and the joy of the singing,
Swept peace o'er my hate, and was sweet
As the freshness the waters were bringing
Was cool to my desert-baked feet.

" Thereon I raised mine enemy, and gave
The cold clear water of the wave ;
And when he blessed me I did give again,
And had strange fear my bounty were but vain;
When, as I bent, he smote me through the breast.
And that is all !   Great Allah knows the rest."

Said Nekkeer, the clerk of man's wrong,
"Great Solomon's self might be long
In judging this mad son of song."

Cried the poet, "Shall two men agree?
Thou mighty collector of sin,
Be advised, come with me to the Inn;
There are friends who shall witness for me.
Great-bellied, respectable, stanch,
One arm set a-crook on the haunch,
They will pour the red wine of advice;
And behold, ye shall know in a trice
How hopeless of wisdom to weigh
The song words a poet may say."

Said Nekkeer, the clerk of ill thought,
"Ah! where shall decision be sought?
Let us quit the crazed maker of verse,
A confuser of good and of worse."

"But first," quoth this Attar El Din,
"I am dry; leave my soul at the Inn."

Newport, *October*, 1891.

How gentle here is Nature's mood!  She lays
  A woman-hand upon the troubled heart,
  Bidding the world away and time depart,
While the brief minutes swoon to endless days
Filled full of sad, inconstant thoughtfulness.

Behold 't is eventide.  Dun cattle stand
  Drowsed in the misted grasses.  From the
      hollows deep,
  Dim veils, adrift, o'er arch and tower sweep,
Casting a dreary doubt along the land,
Weighting the twilight with some vague dis-
      tress.

Transient and subtle, not to thought more near
  Than spirit is to flesh, about me rise
  Dim memories, long lost to love's sad eyes ;
Now are they wandering shadows, strange and
      drear,
That from their natal substance far have strayed.

The witches of the mind possess the time,
  And cry, " Behold thy dead ! "  They come,
    they pass ;
We yearn to give them feature, face.  Alas!
Love hath no morn for memory's failing prime ;
What once was sweet with truth is but a shade.

The ghosts of nameless sorrow, joy, despair,
  Emotions that have no remembered source,
  Love-waifs from other worlds, hope, fear, re-
    morse
Born of some vision's crime, wail through the air,
Crying, We were and are not, — that is all.

Yet sweet the indecisive evening hour
  That hath of earth the least.  Unreal as
    dreams
  Dreamed within dreams, and ever further,
    seems
The sound of human toil, while grass and flower
Bend where the mercy of the dew doth fall.

Strange mysteries of expectation wait
  Above the grave-mounds of the storied space,
  Where, buried, lie a nation's strength and
    grace,

And the sad joys of Rome's imperious state
That perished of its insolent excess.

A dull, gray shroud o'er this vast burial rests,
  Is deathly still, or seems to rise and fall,
   As on a dear one, dead, the moveless pall
Doth cheat the heart with stir of her white
       breasts,
Mocking the troubled hour with worse distress.

A deathful languor holds the twilight mist,
  Unearthly colors drape the Alban hills,
   A dull malaria the spirit fills ;
Death and decay all beauty here have kissed,
Pledging the land to sorrowing loveliness.

ROME, *May*, 1891.

# THE PROTESTANT CEMETERY AT ROME

## THE GRAVE OF KEATS

"Here lies one whose name was writ in water." [1]

FAIR little city of the pilgrim dead,
Dear are thy marble streets, thy rosy lanes:
Easy it seems and natural here to die,
And death a mother, who with tender care
Doth lay to sleep her ailing little ones.
Old are these graves, and they who, mournfully,
Saw dust to dust return, themselves are
        mourned;
Yet, in green cloisters of the cypress shade,
Full-choired chants the fearless nightingale
Ancestral songs learned when the world was
        young.
Sing on, sing ever in thy breezy homes;
Toss earthward from the white acacia bloom
The mingled joy of fragrance and of song;
Sing in the pure security of bliss.

[1] Inscription placed on his tomb, at Keats's request.

These dead concern thee not, nor thee the fear
That is the shadow of our earthly loves.
And me thou canst not comfort; tender hearts
Inherit here the anguish of the doubt
Writ on this gravestone.  He, at last, I trust,
Serenity of confident attainment knows.
The night falls, and the darkened verdure starred
With pallid roses shuts the world away.
Sad wandering souls of song, frail ghosts of
       thought
That voiceless died, the massing shadows haunt,
Troubling the heart with unfulfilled delight.
The moon is listening in the vault of heaven,
And, like the airy march of mighty wings,
The rhythmic throb of stately cadences
Inthralls the ear with some high-measured
       verse,
Where ecstasies of passion-nurtured words
For great thoughts find a home, and fill the
       mind
With echoes of divinely purposed hopes
That wore on earth the death-pall of despair.
Night darkens round me.  Never more in life
May I, companioned by the friendly dead,
Walk in this sacred fellowship again;

Therefore, thou silent singer 'neath the grass,
Sing to me still those sweeter songs unsung,
" Pipe to the spirit ditties of no tone,"
Caressing thought with wonderments of phrase
Such as thy springtide rapture knew to win.
Ay, sing to me thy unborn summer songs,
And the ripe autumn lays that might have been ;
Strong wine of fruit mature, whose flowers alone
      we know.

Rome, *May*, 1891.

Ripe hours there be that do anticipate
   The heritage of death, and bid us see,
   As from the vantage of eternity,
The shadow-symbols of historic fate.

As o'er some Alpine summit's lonely steep,
   Blinding and terrible with spears of light,
   Hurling the snows from many a shaken height,
The storm-clad spirits of the mountain sweep, —

Thus, in the solitude where broodeth thought,
   Torn from rent chasms of the soundless past,
   Go by me, as if borne upon the blast,
The awful forms which time and man have
      wrought.

Swift through the gloom each mournful chariot
      rolls,
   Dim shapes of empire urge the flying steeds,

Featured with man's irrevocable deeds,
Robed with the changeful passions of men's
    souls.

Ethereal visions pass serene in prayer,
    Their eyes aglow with sacrificial light ;
    Phantoms of creeds long dead, their garments
        bright,
Drip red with blood of torture and despair.

In such an hour my spirit did behold
    A woman wonderful.  Unnumbered years
    Left in her eyes the beauty born of tears,
And full they were of fatal stories old.

The trophies of her immemorial reign
    The shadowy great of eld beside her bore ;
    A broidery of ancient song she wore,
And the glad muses held her regal train.

Still hath she kingdom o'er the souls of men ;
    Dear is she always in her less estate.
    The sad, the gay, the thoughtful, on her wait,
Praising her evermore with tongue and pen.

Stately her ways and sweet, and all her own ;
   As one who has forgotten time she lives,
   Loves, loses, lures anew, and ever gives, —
She who all misery and all joy hath known.

If thou wouldst see her, as the twilight fails,
   Go forth along the ancient street of tombs,
   And when the purple shade divinely glooms
High o'er the Alban hills, and night prevails,

If then she is not with thee while the light
   Glows over roof and column, tower and dome,
   And the dead stir beneath thy feet, and Rome
Lies in the solemn keeping of the night, —

If then she be not thine, not thine the lot
   Of those some angel rescues for an hour
   From earth's mean limitations, granting power
To see as man may see when time is not.

  Rome, *May*, 1891.

# MY LADY OF THE ROSES

At Venice, while the twilight hour
    Yet lit a gray-walled garden space,
    I saw a woman fair of face
Pass, as in thought, from flower to flower.
    The roses, haply, something said,
    For here and there she bent her head,
Till, startled from their hidden nest
In the covert of her breast,
    Blushes rose, like fluttered birds,
    At those naughty rosy words.
One need not wise as Portia be
To guess love held her heart in fee.
    Prudently a full-blown rose
    For her confidence she chose:
Whispering, she took its breath,
And, for what its fragrance saith,
    Smiling knelt, and kissed it twice;
    Caught it, held it, kissed it thrice.
Ah! her kiss the rose had killed;
    Wrecked, in tender disarray

On the ground its petals lay,
All its autumn fate fulfilled.
  Swiftly from her paling face
  Fell the rosy flush apace.
Had her kiss recalled a bliss
Life for evermore should miss?
  Had there been a fatal hour
  When false lips had hurt the flower
Of love, and now its sad estate
She saw in that dead rose's fate?
  Who may know? A little while
  She lingered with a doubtful smile;
Took then a younger rose, whose slips
The garden knew, and with her lips
  Its color matched. What gracious words
  It said might know the garden birds, —
Something, perchance, that liked her well;
But roses kiss, and never tell.

  What confession, what dear boon,
  Heard that ruddy priest of June?
Was it a mad gypsy-rose
Fortunes eager to disclose,
  Gravely whispering predictions
  Rich with love's unending fictions,

Saying nonsense good to hear,
Like a pleasant-mannered seer?
  Gypsy palms are crossed with gold,
  But my lady, gayly bold,
In the antique coin of kisses
Paid for prophecy of blisses;
  And, to make assurance sure,
  This conspirator demure
Murmured, in a pretty way,
What her prophet ought to say.
  Low she laughed, and then was gone;
  My pleasant little play was done.

Alone I sit and muse.   Below,
Black gondolas glide to and fro,
  Like shadows that have stolen away
  From centuried arch and palace gray.
Then, as if out of memory brought,
  The sequel of my garden masque
Comes silently, by fancy wrought, —
  A gift I had not cared to ask.

Lo! where the terraced marble ends,
  Barred by the sweetbrier's scented bound,
The lady of my dream descends,

And day by day the garden ground
Her footsteps know; with lingering gait,
She wanders early, wanders late,
    Or, sadly patient, on the lawn
Each day renews her gentle trust,
    When, from the busy highway drawn,
Float high its curves of sunlit dust.
        The children of her garden greet
        With counsel innocent and sweet
        The coming of her constant feet.
She whispers, and their low replies
Bring gladness to her lips and eyes;
        She will no other company;
        For her the flowers have come to be
        All of life's dimmed reality.
Purple pansies, gold embossed,
That in love had once been crossed,
Murmur, We have loved and lost;
        And the cool blue violets
        Sigh, We wait for life's regrets.
Thistles gray, beyond the fence,
Mutter prickly common sense;
        While the lilies, pale and bent,
        Say, We too sinned, are penitent;
        Only that can bring content.

Red generations of the rose
Unheeded passed to death's repose ;
   The peach upon the crumbling wall,
   With springtide bloom and autumn fall,
No proverb had to foster fear,
No time-born wisdom brought her near.
   The willows o'er two noisy brooks,
   In marriage come to sober mood,
Were but green slips, that eve of May ;
Now, underneath their shade she looks,
   And smiling says, " Time must be rude,
To keep him thus so many a day."
They tell her he is dead ! " Ah ! nay,"
She answers ; " he but rode away,
And he will come again in May.
   And I can wait," she says, and stands
   With roses in her thin white hands.
Childlike, with innocent replies,
She meets the world. Wide open lies
   Her book of life ; Time turns the leaves,
   Like each to each, because she grieves
Nor less nor more, save when in fear,
On one dark eve of all the year,
   Dismayed lest love's divine distress
   Be dulled by time's forgetfulness.

VENICE, *June*, 1891.

# THE QUAKER LADY [1]

'MID drab and gray of mouldered leaves,
  The spoil of last October,
I see the Quaker lady stand
  In dainty garb and sober.

No speech has she for praise or prayer,
  No blushes, as I claim
To know what gentle whisper gave
  Her prettiness a name.

The wizard stillness of the hour
  My fancy aids : again
Return the days of hoop and hood
  And tranquil William Penn.

I see a maid amid the wood
  Demurely calm and meek,
Or troubled by the mob of curls
  That riots on her cheek.

[1] *Oldenlandia cærulea* (bluets, innocence), known in Pennsylvania as the " Quaker ladies."

(34)

Her eyes are blue, her cheeks are red, —
  Gay colors for a Friend, —
And Nature with her mocking rouge
  Stands by a blush to lend.

The gown that holds her rosy grace
  Is truly of the oddest;
And wildly leaps her tender heart
  Beneath the kerchief modest.

It must have been the poet Love
  Who, while she slyly listened,
Divined the maiden in the flower,
  And thus her semblance christened.

Was he a proper Quaker lad
  In suit of simple gray?
What fortune had his venturous speech,
  And was it " yea " or " nay "?

And if indeed she murmured " yea,"
  And throbbed with worldly bliss,
I wonder if in such a case
  Do Quakers really kiss?

Or was it some love-wildered beau
    Of old colonial days,
With clouded cane and broidered coat,
    And very artful ways?

And did he whisper through her curls
    Some wicked, pleasant vow,
And swear no courtly dame had words
    As sweet as " thee " and " thou " ?

Or did he praise her dimpled chin
    In eager song or sonnet,
And find a merry way to cheat
    Her kiss-defying bonnet ?

And sang he then in verses gay,
    Amid this forest shady,
The dainty flower at her feet
    Was like his Quaker lady?

And did she pine in English fogs,
    Or was his love enough?
And did she learn to sport the fan,
    And use the patch and puff ?

Alas! perhaps she played quadrille,
  And, naughty grown and older,
Was pleased to show a dainty neck
  Above a snowy shoulder.

But sometimes in the spring, I think,
  She saw, as in a dream,
The meeting-house, the home sedate,
  The Schuylkill's quiet stream;

And sometimes in the minuet's pause
  Her heart went wide afield
To where, amid the woods of May,
  A blush its love revealed.

Till far away from court and king
  And powder and brocade,
The Quaker ladies at her feet
  Their quaint obeisance made.

NEWPORT, 1889.

# THE WRECK OF THE EMMELINE [1]

THIS tack might fetch Absecom bar,
  The wind lies fair for the Dancin' Jane ;
She 's good on a wind.   If we keep this way,
  You might talk with folk in the land of Spain.

A tidy snack of a breeze it be ;
  Just hear it whistle 'mong them dunes !
It ain't no more nor a gal for strong, —
  Sakes ! but it hollers a lot of toones.

Ye 'd ought to hear it October-time
  A-fiddlin' 'mong them cat-tails tall ;
Our Bill can fiddle, but 'gainst that wind
  He ain't no kind of a show at all.

Respectin' the wrack you want to see,
  It 's yon away, set hard and fast
On the outer bar.   When tides is low
  You kin see a mawsel of rib an' mast.

[1] A true story.

(38)

Four there was on us, wrackers all,
  Born and bred to foller the sea,
And Dad beside ; that 's him you seed
  Las' night a-mendin' them nets with me.

Waal, sir, it was n't no night for talk ;
  The pipes went out, an' we stood, we four,
A-starin' dumb through the rattlin' panes,
  And says Tom, " I 'd as lief be here ashore."

The wust wind ever I knowed
  Was swoopin' across the deep,
An' the waves was humpin' as white as snow,
  An' gallopin' in like frighted sheep.

Says Bill, " 'T ain't nat'ral, that big moon
  Ed be so quiet, them stars that bright,
A-p'intin' down from the big old roof,
  As they might be icicles tipt with light."

Lord ! sich a wind ! It tuk that sand
  An' flung it squar' on the winder-sash,
An' howled and mumbled 'mong the scrub,
  An' yelled like a hurt thing 'cross the mash.

Old Dad as was sittin' 'side the fire ;
  Jus' now an' agin he riz his head,
An' says he, " God help all folks at sea, —
  God help 'em livin', and bury 'em dead.

"God help them in smacks as sail,
  An' men as v'yage in cruisers tall ;
God help all as goes by water,
  Big ship and little, — help 'em all."

" Amen !" says Bill, jus' like it was church ;
  An' all of a sudden says Joe to me,
" Hallo !" an' thar' was a flash of light,
  An' the roar of a gun away to sea.

" An' it 's each for all !" cries Dad to me ;
  " The night ain't much of a choice for sweet."
So up he jumps an' stamps aroun',
  Jus' for to waken his sleepy feet.

" An' it 's into ilers and on with boots,"
  Sings Dad, " Thar' be n't no time to spar'.
Pull in y'r waist-straps.   Hurry a bit ;
  The shortest time 'll be long out thar'."

I did n't like it, nor them no more,
  But roun' we scuttles for oar and ropes,
An' out we plunged in the old man's wake,
  For we knowed as we was thar' only hopes.

The door druv' in; the cinders flew;
  The house, it shook; out went the light;
The air was thick with squandered sand,
  As nipt like the sting of a bluefly bite.

We passed yon belt of holly and pine,
  An' in among them cedar an' oak
We stood a bit on the upper shore,
  An' stared an' listened, but no man spoke.

" Whar' lies she, Bill?" roars Dad to me,
  As down we bended. Then bruk' a roar
As follered a lane of dancin' light
  That flashed and fluttered along the shore.

" She 's thar'," says Joe; " I 'd sight of her
    then;
  She 's hard and high on the outer bar.
Nary a light, and fast enough,
  And nary a mawsel of mast or spar."

Groans Dad, " Good Lord, it 's got to be ! "
   Says Tom, " It ain't to be done, I fear."
Shouts Joe, a-laffin' (he allus laffed),
   " It ain't to be done by standin' here."

Waal, in she went, third time of tryin', —
   " In with a will," laffs Joe, in a roar,
Wind a-cussin' and Dad a-prayin',
   But spry enough with the steerin' oar.

Five hours — an' cold.   I was clean played out.
   " Give way," shouts Dad, " give way thar'
      now ! "
" Hurray ! " laffs Joe.   An' we slung her along,
   With a prayer to aft an' a laff in the bow.

There was five men glad when we swep' her in
   Under the lee, an' none too soon.
" Aboard thar', mates!" shouts Dad, an' the
      wind
   Jus' howled like a dog at full of moon.

" Up with you, Bill ! " sung Dad.   So I —
   I grabbed for a broken rope as hung.
Gosh ! it was stiff as an anchor-stock,
   But up I swarmed, and over I swung.

Ice ?  She was ice from stem to starn.
 I gripped the rail an' sarched the wrack,
An' cleared my eyes, an' sarched agin'
 For livin' sign on that slidin' deck.


 Four dead men in the scuppers lay
  Stiff as steel, they was froze that fast ;
An' one old man was hangin' awry,
  Tied to the stump of the broken mast.


Ice-bound he were.  But he kinder smiled,
 A-lookin' up.  I was sort of skeered.
Lord! thinks I, thar' was many a prayer
 Froze in the snow of that orful beard.


Thar' was one man lashed to the wheel,
 An' his eyes was a-starin' wild,
An' thar', close-snuggled up in his arms, —
 O Lord, sir, the pity ! — a little child.


Now that jus' done for me.  Down I fell,
 Jus' fell to my knees, — I das n't stand, —
An' I says, " O Lord ! the wicked wind,
 It has killed at sea an' cussed on land."

Then a leap to the boat.  " Dead all," says I ;
  " Give way," an' we bent to the springin' oar ;
An' never no word says boy or Dad,
  Till we crashed full high on the upper shore.

Then Dad, he dropped for to pray,
  But I stood all a shake on the sand ;
An' the old man says, " I could wish them souls
  Was fetched ashore to the joyful land."

But Joe, he laffs.  Says Dad, right mad,
  " Shut up.  Ye 'd grin if ye went to heaven."
" Why  not ? " says Joe.  " As  for  this  here
      earth,
  It takes lots of laffin' to keep things even."

Ready about, an' mind for the boom ;
  Ef ye keer for to hold that far,
You may see the Emmeline, keel and rib,
  Stuck fast an' firm on the outer bar.

NEWPORT, *October*, 1891.

# VENICE

I am Venezia, that sad Magdalen,
  Who with her lovers' arms the turbaned East
Smote, and through lusty centuries of gain
  Lived a wild queen of battle and of feast.
I netted, in gold meshes of my hair,
  The great of soul; painter and poet, priest,
Bent at my will with picture, song, and prayer,
And ever love of me their fame increased,
    Till I, a queen, became the slave of slaves,
      And, like the ghost-kings of the Umbrian
        plain,
    Saw from my centuries torn, as from their
      graves,
The priceless jewels of my haughty reign.
    Gone are my days of gladness, now in vain
I hurt the tender with my speechless pain.

Venice, *June*, 1891.

## VENICE TO ITALY

O ITALY, thou fateful mistress-land,
   That, like Delilah, won with deathful bliss
   Each conquering foe who wooed thy wanton
      kiss,
And sheared thy lovers' strength with certain
      hand,
And gave them to Philistia's bonds of vice;
   Smiling to see the strong limbs waste away,
   The manly vigor crippled by decay,
Usurious years exact the minute's price.
Ah! when *my* great were greatest, ever glad,
   I thanked them with the hope of nobler
      deeds.
   Statesman and poet, painter, sculptor,
      knight, —
These my dear lovers were ere days grew sad,
   And them I taught how mightily exceeds
   All other love the love that holds God's light.

VENICE, *June,* 1891.

(46)

# THE DECAY OF VENICE

The glowing pageant of my story lies,
  A shaft of light across the stormy years,
  When 'mid the agony of blood and tears,
Or pope or kaiser won the mournful prize,
Till I, the fearless child of ocean, heard
  The step of doom, and trembling to my fall,
Remorseful knew that I had seen unstirred
  Proud Freedom's death, the tyrant's festival ;
    Whilst that Italia which was yet to be,
And is, and shall be, sat a virgin pure,
High over Umbria on the mountain slopes,
    And saw the failing fires of liberty
  Fade on the chosen shrine she deemed secure,
When died for many a year man's noblest hopes.

VENICE, *June*, 1891.

# PISA: THE DUOMO

Lo, this is like a song writ long ago,
  Born of the easy strength of simpler days,
  Filled with the life of man, his joy, his praise,
Marriage and childhood, love, and sin, and woe,
Defeat and victory, and all men know
  Of passionate remorses, and the stays
  That help the weary on life's rugged ways.
A dreaming seraph felt this beauty grow
    In sleep's pure hour, and with joy grown
      bold
Set the fair crystal in the thought of man;
And Time, with antique tints of ivory wan,
  And gentle industries of rain and light,
    Its stones rejoiced, and o'er them crumbled
      gold
  Won from the boundaries of day and night.

PISA, *May*, 1891.

(48)

# THE VESTAL'S DREAM

Ah, Venus, white-limbed mother of delight,
  Why shouldst thou tease her with a dream so
    dear?
  Winged tenderness of kisses, hovering near,
Her gentle longings cheat.  Forbidden sight
Of eager eyes doth through the virgin night
  Perplex her innocence with cherished fear.
  O cruel thou, with sweets to ripen here
In wintry cloisters what can know but blight.
    Wilt leave her now to scorn?  The lictor's
      blows
To-morrow shall be merciless.  The light
Dies on the altar!  Nay, swift through the night,
  Comes pitiful the queen of young desire,
    That reddened in a dream this chaste white
      rose,
  And lights with silver torch the fallen fire.

Rome, May, 1891.

# LINCOLN

CHAINED by stern duty to the rock of state,
  His spirit armed in mail of rugged mirth,
  Ever above, though ever near to earth,
Yet felt his heart the vulture beaks that sate
Base appetites, and foul with slander, wait
  Till the keen lightnings bring the awful hour
  When wounds and suffering shall give them
    power.
Most was he like to Luther, gay and great,
  Solemn and mirthful, strong of heart and
    limb.
  Tender and simple too ; he was so near
  To all things human that he cast out fear,
And, ever simpler, like a little child,
  Lived in unconscious nearness unto Him
Who always on earth's little ones hath smiled.

NEWPORT, *October*, 1891.

# THE LOST PHILOPENA

TO M. G. M.

MORE blest is he who gives than who receives,
  For he that gives doth always something get :
  Angelic usurers that interest set :
And what we give is like the cloak of leaves
    Which to the beggared earth the great
      trees fling,
  Thoughtless of gain in chilly Autumn days :
  The mystic husbandry of nature's ways
    Shall fetch it back in greenery of the
      Spring.
One tender gift there is, my little maid,
  That doth the giver and receiver bless,
  And shall with obligation none distress ;
Coin of the heart in God's just balance weighed ;
  Wherefore, sweet spendthrift, still be prodigal,
  And freely squander what thou hast from all.

LUCERNE, *July,* 1891.

# ST. CHRISTOPHER

THERE was none so tall as this giant bold.
He had a name that could not be told,
A name so crooked no Christian men
Could say it over and speak again.
One day he came where a good man prayed
All alone in the forest shade.
Then the giant in wonder said:
" Why do you bend the knee and head ? "
" I bend," he said, " because I be
The weakest thing that you can see.
I pray for help to do no wrong,
To Christ who is so good and strong."
" Ho," said the giant, " when I see
One strong enough to conquer me,
I shall be glad to bend my knees,
Which are as stout as any trees."
" But," said the good man, sad and old,
" Yon stream is deep, the water cold.
Prayer is the Spirit's work for some.

(52)

Work is the prayer of the body dumb."
" If that be prayer," said the giant tall,
" The maimed and sick, the weak and small,
Across the stream and to and fro,
I shall carry and come and go,
Until the time when I shall see
Thy strong Christ come to humble me."
So all day long, with patient hand,
He bore the weak from strand to strand.
At last, one eve, when winds were wild,
He heard the voice of a little child
Saying, " Giant, art thou asleep?
Carry me over the river deep."
On his shoulder broad he set the child,
And laughed to see how the infant smiled.
Up to his waist the giant strode,
While fierce around the water flowed ;
His great back shook, his great knees bent,
As staggering through the waves he went.
" Why is this ?" he cried aloud ;
"Why should my great back be bowed ? "
Spake from his shoulder, sweet and clear,
A voice, — 't was like a bird's to hear, —
" I am the Christ to whom men pray
When comes the morn and wanes the day."

" No," said the giant, " a child art thou.
  Not to a babe shall proud men bow! "
  He set the child on the farther land,
  And wiped his brow with shaking hand.
" In truth," he cried, " the load was great ;
  Wherefore art thou this heavy weight?"
  The little child said, " I was heavy to thee
  Because the world's sins rest on me."
" If thou canst carry them all on thee,
  Who art but a little child to see,
  Thou must be strong, and I be weak,
  And thou must be the one I seek."
  Therefore the giant, day by day,
  Still kept his work, and learned to pray.
  And his pagan name that none should hear,
  Was changed to Giant Christopher.

1887.

# DREAMLAND

Up anchor !   Up anchor !
  Set sail and away!
The ventures of dreamland
  Are thine for a day.
Yo, heave ho !
  Aloft and alow
Elf sailors are singing,
  Yo, heave ho !
The breeze that is blowing
  So sturdily strong
Shall fill up thy sail
  With the breath of a song.
A fay at the mast-head
  Keeps watch o'er the sea ;
Blown amber of tresses
  Thy banner shall be ;
Thy freight the lost laughter
  That sad souls have missed,
Thy cargo the kisses
  That never were kissed.

And ho, for a fay maid
   Born merry in June,
Of dainty red roses
   Beneath a red moon.
The star-pearls that midnight
   Casts down on the sea,
Dark gold of the sunset
   Her fortune shall be.
And ever she whispers,
   More tenderly sweet,
" Love am I, love only,
   Love perfect, complete.
The world is my lordship,
   The heart is my slave ;
I mock at the ages,
   I laugh at the grave.
Wilt sail with me ever,
   A dream-haunted sea,
Whose whispering waters
   Shall murmur to thee
The love-haunted lyrics
   Dead poets have made
Ere life had a fetter,
   Ere love was afraid ? "

Then up with the anchor!
Set sail and away!
The ventures of loveland
Are thine for a day.

NEWPORT, 1890.

# EVENING BY THE SEA

WITH noble waste of lazy hours
I loitered, till I saw the moon,
A rosy pearl, hang vast and strange
Above the long gray dune !

And hither, thither, as I went,
My ancient friend the sea beside,
Whatever tune my spirit sang
The dear old comrade tried.

BAR HARBOR, 1892.

# IDLENESS

THERE is no dearer lover of lost hours
Than I.
I can be idler than the idlest flowers;
More idly lie
Than noonday lilies languidly afloat,
And water pillowed in a windless moat.
And I can be
Stiller than some gray stone
That hath no motion known.
It seems to me
That my still idleness doth make my own
All magic gifts of joy's simplicity.

RESTIGOUCHE RIVER, 1892.

(59)

# A GRAVEYARD

As beats the unrestful sea some ice-clad isle
Set in the sorrowful night of arctic seas,
Some lorn domain of endless silences,
So, echoless, unanswered, falleth here
The great voiced city's roar of fretful life.

Rome, 1891.

(60)

c

# LOSS

LIFE may moult many feathers, yet delight
To soar and circle in a heaven of joy ;
The pinion robbed must learn more swift employ,
Till the thinned feathers end our eager flight.

BAR HARBOR, 1892.

# COME IN

"Come in."  I stand, and know in thought
  The honest kiss, the waiting word,
  The love with friendship interwrought,
  The face serene by welcome stirred.
Bar Harbor, 1892.

# GOOD–NIGHT

GOOD-NIGHT.  Good-night.  Ah, good the night
That wraps thee in its silver light.
Good-night.  No night is good for me
That does not hold a thought of thee.
　　　　Good-night.

Good-night.  Be every night as sweet
As that which made our love complete,
Till that last night when death shall be
One brief " Good-night," for thee and me.
　　　　Good-night.

NEWPORT, 1890.

# THE RISING TIDE

AN idle man I stroll at eve,
   Where move the waters to and fro ;
Full soon their added gains will leave
   Small space for me to come and go.

Already in the clogging sand,
   I walk with dull, retarded feet;
Yet still is sweet the lessening strand,
   And still the lessening light is sweet.

NEWPORT, *October*, 1891.

# VERSES

READ ON THE PRESENTATION BY S. WEIR MITCHELL
TO THE PHILADELPHIA COLLEGE OF PHYSICIANS OF
SARAH W. WHITMAN'S PORTRAIT OF OLIVER WEN-
DELL HOLMES, M. D.

WE call them great who have the magic art
To summon tears and stir the human heart,
With fictive grief to bring the soul annoy,
And leave a dew-drop in the rose of joy.
A nobler purpose had the Masters wise
Who from your walls look down with kindly
      eyes.
Theirs the firm hand and theirs the ready brain
Strong for the battle with disease and pain.
Large were their lives : these scholars, gentle,
      brave,
Knew all of man from cradle unto grave.
What note of torment had they failed to hear ?
All grief's stern gamut knew each pitying ear.
Nor theirs the useless sympathy that stands

Beside the suffering with defenseless hands;
Divinely wise, their pity had the art
To teach the brain the ardour of the heart.
These left a meaner for a nobler George;
These trod the red snows by the Valley Forge,
Saw the wild birth-throes of a nation's life,
The long-drawn misery and the doubtful strife:
Yea, and on darker fields they left their dead
Where grass-grown streets heard but the bear-
    er's tread,
While the sad death-roll of those fatal days
Left small reward beyond the poor man's praise.
Lo! Shadowy greetings from each canvas come,
Lips seem to move now for a century dumb:
From tongues long hushed the sound of welcome
    falls,
" Place, place for Holmes upon these honoured
    walls."
The lights are out, the festal flowers fade,
Our guests are gone, the great hall wrapped in
    shade.
Lone in the midst this silent picture stands,
Ringed with the learning of a score of lands.
From dusty tomes in many a tongue I hear
A gentle Babel,—" Welcome, Brother dear.

Yea, though Apollo won thy larger hours,
And stole our fruit, and only left us flowers,
The poet's rank thy title here completes —
Doctor and Poet, — so were Goldsmith, —
  Keats."
The voices failing murmur to an end
With "Welcome, Doctor, Scholar, Poet, Friend."

In elder days of quiet wiser folks,
When the great Hub had not so many spokes,
Two wandering Gods, upon the Common, found
A weary schoolboy sleeping on the ground.
Swift to his brain their eager message went,
Swift to his heart each ardent claim was sent;
" Be mine," Minerva cried. " This tender hand
Skilled in the art of arts shall understand
With magic touch the demon pain to lay.
From skill to skill and on to clearer day
Far through the years shall fare that ample
  brain
To read the riddles of disease and pain."
" Nay, mine the boy," Apollo cried aloud,
" His the glad errand, beautiful and proud,
To wing the arrows of delightful mirth,
To slay with jests the sadder things of earth.

At his gay science melancholy dies,
At his clear laugh each morbid fancy flies.
Rich is the quiver I shall give his bow,
The eagle's pinion some bold shafts shall know;
Swift to its mark the angry arrow-song
Shall find the centre of a nation's wrong;
Or in a people's heart one tingling shot
Pleads not in vain against the war-ship's lot.
Yea, I will see that for a gentler flight
The dove's soft feathers send his darts aright
When smiles and pathos, kindly wedded, chant
The plaintive lay of that unmarried aunt;
Or sails his Nautilus the sea of time,
Blown by the breezes of immortal rhyme,
Or with a Godspeed from her poet's brain,
Sweet Clémence trips adown the Rue de Seine.
The humming-bird shall plume the quivering
      song,
Blithe, gay, and restless, never dull or long,
Where gayly passionate his soul is set
To sing the Katydid's supreme regret,
Or creaking jokes, through never-ending days,
Rolls the quaint story of the Deacon's chaise.
Away with tears! When this glad poet sings,
The angel Laughter spreads her broadest wings,

By land and sea where'er St. George's cross
And the starred banner in the breezes toss,
The merry music of his wholesome mirth
Sends rippling smiles around our English earth."

" Not mine," Minerva cried, " to spoil thy joy ;
Divide the honours, — let us share the boy ! "

*April*, 1892.